SPACE KID:
FALLEN ALLIES

by William Kelleher

RoseDog Books
PITTSBURGH, PENNSYLVANIA 15238

RoseDog Books
585 Alpha Drive, Suite 103
Pittsburgh, PA 15238
Visit our website at *www.rosedogbookstore.com*

ISBN: 979-8-88925-181-1
eISBN: 979-8-88925-681-6

Space Kid:
Fallen Allies

Chapter 1

Sweat poured down Space Kid's face. He, Ninja Penguin, and Turtle Boy were in front of Satan himself. Deaddangle, Arctic Wolf, and Shark Boy were up there with Satan.

"You're never going to get away with this, you deranged lunatic!" Space Kid shouted.

"I already did!" Satan boomed. He snapped his fingers and as if they were hypnotized, the villains shouted, "ALL HAIL SATAN! ALL HAIL SATAN!"

"Ninja Penguin, NOW!" Turtle Boy shouted. Ninja Penguin shot Satan in the face with ice. Space Kid and Turtle Boy got the other villains who were recovering from their hypnotic state and Space Kid radioed his ship.

"Space Pig, start the engines!" Space Kid got on board, put the villains in the cell, headed up to the cockpit, and flew away.

Chapter 2

"**W**here should we take these idiots and hide?" Space Kid asked.

"How about The Turtle?" Turtle Boy asked.

"No. My ship can't go in the water," Space Kid said.

"How about the South Pole?" Ninja Penguin asked.

"Okay," Space Kid agreed. His ship flew over Midtown Manhattan as Space Kid turned around the *Bullet*. People on the streets below looked up and stared at Space Kid's ship in fear as it passed by. After the turn, Space Kid got up to head to the mess deck.

"Space Pig, take the wheel, please. Keep us on track to the South Pole," Space Kid said.

"Alright. Also, should I put on Arctic gear?" Space Pig asked.

"Yeah, go ahead. Also, keep a steady 460-575 mph speed," said Space Kid. Space Kid went to the mess deck to brief the troops.

"Alright, gentlemen. We will arrive at the South Pole in about eighteen and a half hours. Until then take anything you like from the mini bar, relax, go to bed, roam around, do anything, I don't care!" Space Kid stated. Eighteen and a half hours later, the *Bullet* landed at the South Pole.

"Ninja Penguin, open up the base. Then we'll move our equipment in. This is where we are staying for the next few months. Until Mindwave can clear our names," Space Kid said. Space Kid walked outside the *Bullet* and stood in the cold snow.

"Storm's coming! Better get inside!" Ninja Penguin warned. He sent the warning to the penguins to get inside the South Pole. Everyone got everything inside the base just as the storm hit. Space Kid flew the *Bullet* into the hangar of the base. He got out and said, "Time to get some help."

CHAPTER 3

Far away on the dwarf planet Pluto, a small *PING* went off on someone's wrist communicator.

"Hey, Space Kid! What do you need?" the mysterious speaker asked.

"Adventurer, I need you and Crusher to come to the South Pole," Space Kid said.

"Danger Boy! Get over here! You too, Crusher! Crusher and I were summoned by Space Kid to head to the South Pole base of Ninja Penguin. Crusher, get in the gunner seat. Danger Boy, you're in command," the Adventurer said. They took off on the spaceship and light jumped back to Earth.

"Well, we're here," Crusher said.

"Unidentified ship, who are you?" Ninja Penguin asked.

"Backup, requesting permission to land in Hangar Five," the Adventurer stated. They landed in the South Pole at the site of a penguin buffing the floor. They walked to the main office just as an alarm blared.

"Turtle Boy, get to the south gun, I'll take the north. Space Kid catch them in the air!" Ninja Penguin yelled. Space Kid hopped into a Penguin Speeder and flew off.

"Squad Seven, fall back and protect the base, Squads One, Two, Three, and Four follow me, Squad Five takes the east, Squad Six takes the west," Space Kid commanded.

"Time to make the enemy out of us that the world thinks we are!" Space Pig said. *Boom! Boom! Boom! Boom! Boom! Boom! Boom! Boom!* Turtle Boy fired his gun. *Boom! Boom! Boom! Boom! Boom! Boom! Boom! Boom!* Ninja Penguin did the same. Space Kid and Space Pig shot down multiple planes, and so did the penguins. "They're retreating!" yelled Space Pig.

"Fall back," Space Kid ordered. The Flying Penguins all flew back into the hangar after another victory.

CHAPTER 4

LATER THAT DAY, THE SIX HEROES WERE WATCHING THE NEWS.

"In a not-so-stunning turn of events today, the UN's fallen allies, Space Kid, Space Pig, Ninja Penguin, and Turtle Boy attacked UN explorers who got too close to their base. Here's what expedition leader General O'Leary of the United States of America had to say, 'Space Kid and his allies are not to be trusted. They are now wanted criminals who, if they ever show their faces again, will be shot on sight. If—"

"Hey!" Turtle Boy said as Space Kid turned off the TV.

"That's enough for tonight," Space Kid stated. He walked out of the room and went outside of the base. On the way, he passed Gerald the Penguin, who was still buffing the floor.

"Hey, bud," Ninja Penguin said.

"Hey, Ninja Penguin. Sorry about what happened inside," Space Kid replied. "Have you ever felt this powerless? That this is the one villain we can't beat? I can't die, and Space Pig can't die either, but you and Turtle Boy can. I can't live knowing that I was the witness to your murders."

"William, we both know that it won't happen. It's the US. They lie all the time," Ninja Penguin said. Space Kid looked at his watch.

"Adam. I just got news from our Swiss intelligence. Switzerland is still on our side. We don't have to stay at the South Pole for a few months," Space Kid said excitedly.

"Alright! I'll tell everyone the news," Ninja Penguin said. A few hours later, the *Bullet* and the *Adventure I* set off from the South Pole.

"Keep your cloaking devices on until we get into Swiss airspace," Space Kid radioed the Adventurer.

"There's something you don't see every day," said Space Pig pointing at the giant sign saying, "WILLKOMMEN WELTRAUMKIND, WELRAUM-SCHWEIN, NINJA PINGUIN, UND SCHILDKRÖTENJUNGE!"

"WOBOTO, what does that sign say in A English?" Turtle Boy asked.

"It says, 'Welcome Space Kid, Space Pig, Ninja Penguin, and Turtle Boy' in German," WOBOTO said.

Chapter 5

Somewhere in the Atlantic Ocean, the Turtle was sitting waiting for a mission. Some turtles were playing seven-card poker. The dealer was Boxer Turtle, Turtle Boy's oldest turtle. At the table was Chomper, Rocky, Apollo, Speedy, Slow Poke, Truck, Big Boy, and Little T.

"INCOMING VIDEO MESSAGE FROM: TURTLE BOY!"

"Hey, Boxer! You guys are playing poker, aren't you? I told Space Kid not to teach you guys. Anyways, we are in Switzerland. So come here ASAP."

Chapter 6

"I can't take this anymore!" Space Kid yelled. "I have to go." Space Kid flew off to Washington DC.

CRASH!

"What the fu—" General O'Leary started.

ZAP!

He fell flat on the floor.

"Shoot me. I dare you," Space Kid yelled at a soldier.

"Okay," said the soldier. *BANG! BANG! BANG! BANG! BANG!* The gunpowder settled and there was Space Kid. *CRACK! BOOM!* Thunder roared. Lightning flashed. O'Leary was getting to his feet.

"Make one move and I'll obliterate all of America!" Space Kid screamed to O'Leary.

"We'll never bow down to you! You will die eventually! We have your weakness! Patriotism!"

"My country gave up on me! I won't die, but you will!" Space Kid shouted. His eyes glowed red. *BOOM!*

Space Kid's eyes snapped open. Sweat ran down his face. His heart was pounding. *It was all a dream,* he thought. Then he remembered he could see the future, and his panic started again. Space Kid flew off to Washington DC.

"Wait! Time to go invisible," Space Kid said.

"Our nuke will land here. Then, we invaded Canada. Then Russia, China, North and South Korea, all of Asia, Europe, Australia, Africa. Then, Antarctica, we'll leave South America alone," General O'Leary said.

"Not if I have anything to say about it!" Space Kid yelled. He reappeared and socked O'Leary in the jaw.

"Playtime's over, jerks," a voice said. Space Pig appeared from the shadows.

"Didn't think I'd let you have all the fun, did you?" Space Pig asked.

"No, I guess I didn't." Space Kid smirked.

"Argh!" Space Kid and Space Pig shouted in unison. The two of them fell into a deep sleep. They awoke in a prison cell.

"Well. look who decided to awake," O'Leary stated.

"You're corrupt!" Space Pig told him.

"That's why your men keep dying in battle. You're throwing battles. I can't believe this. A few years ago, I served in your ranks in Mexico. You were a military genius. What happened to you?" Space Kid asked.

"I happened to him!" Satan shouted. "After you attacked my base, I manipulated everyone's minds to believe you were evil. I also had the idea to corrupt your former general." Just then Ninja Penguin, Turtle Boy, the Adventurer, Crusher, the Penguin Forces, and the Grand Army of Turtlelandia arrived.

"How! I stripped you of all of your communication devices!" Satan yelled.

"Where you shot me, that's my in-suit tracker," Space Kid calmly stated.

"Time to go to work!" Space Kid yelled. Suddenly it was only Space Kid and Satan in a white void.

"Who are you?" Space Kid asked.

"I'm you. From the future. Of an alternate dimension. In a parallel universe," said Satan.

"That vision of the future, was that of you?" Space Kid asked.

"Yes. I destroyed my universe, so I went back in time to alternate realities to destroy others," Satan said.

"I'm just going to go past the fact you tried to destroy the entire universe, which I'm still pissed off about, but you're saying there's a multiverse. I mean, I tried to open that gateway before, but how did you do it?" asked Space Kid.

"Well, I—"

WHAM!

"That's for being a jerk," said Space Kid. Reality came back into focus, just as the Battle of the Pentagon was ending. Space Kid was zapped up to the Penguin Transfer Ship and went to the barracks. Space Pig was already there.

"WTF happened to you? You look like you just saw a ghost?" Space Pig asked.

"Bud, I have seen ghosts before, remember Hell. It's nothing *Nothing* for you to make a fuss about," Space Kid stated as he laid on the bunk.

"Mister Space Kid, the doctor will see you now," a Medical Penguin said.

"What did he say, Space Kid?" asked Space Pig.

"Nothing. All I know is that my translation device works."

Chapter 7

Hours after his physical, Space Kid went back to his bunk.

"We're now not allowed in Switzerland. Your ships are now in our hangar," Ninja Penguin stated.

"Alright. How about we go to the Moon Outpost now that we have nowhere else to go?" the Adventurer asked.

"It's still open? I thought they shut it down!" Space Kid yelled.

"Yeah it's still open, where do you think I got the hot chocolate and doughnuts from?" the Adventurer asked.

The heroes loaded up their ships to head to the Moon Outpost. Once there, Space Kid got out of his ship and was confronted by Massacre, the leader of the Federation Armed Forces.

"What the hell did you do?" Massacre asked.

"I did nothing," Space Kid yelled.

"Well, you must have done something!" In a rage, Space Kid clenched his fists, until, *WHAM!* He sucker-punched Massacre in the jaw.

"News flash, you're fired. Turtle Boy, congrats, you're now the leader of the Federation Armed Forces," Space Kid stated.

"Thank you, Space Kid," Turtle Boy stated.

"Prepare the troops, sound the alarms, and get me a root beer. This whole thing is about to get much worse," Space Kid acknowledged.

Chapter 8

Turtle Boy looked out at the planet. He remembered becoming a hero and without releasing what he had done, joining Space Kid, his brother, two years ago in his fight against crime, both on Earth and inter-galactically through the Federation. He sat and wondered for a while until Ninja Penguin entered the room.

"Hey, NP. Do you ever wonder why you joined Space Kid?" questioned Turtle Boy.

"No. I felt like it was the right thing to do. Unfortunately, the UN doesn't feel the same way as I do," Ninja Penguin said with a bit of anger.

"Well, I did. Ever since I joined my brother, I've only been suffering. Now everyone in the world hates me," Turtle Boy whimpered.

"Gentleman, we are preparing to make an all-out assault on a new military base in Russia. The Russian government now has enough nuclear warheads to wipe out all of North America. The plan is to get to the base, and I'll grab the nukes, and disarm them in space. Turtle Boy, take the Army and fight; take the Russians prisoners if you have to; Ninja Penguin will lead the Flying Penguins and the Grand Army of Turtlelandia Air Strike Units in a raid of other military bases that were built anytime from the Cold War to the present that might be carrying nukes. Call me to disarm them if there is any. If there aren't, bomb it. Please realize that the UN might try to interfere with this affair, so Turtle Boy you better prepare the Army to have to take more than just Russian forces prisoners. Adventurer and Crusher will keep an eye on O'Leary. Space Pig will go for O'Leary himself. Take him as a prisoner. This mission cannot fail. Good luck, over and out," Space Kid stated.

"Well, this delays my plan by a long bit of time," Turtle Boy sighed.

CHAPTER 9

"**N**OW BOARDING TRANSPORT SHIP 1,234, NOW BOARDING TRANSPORT SHIP 1,234!" a mechanical voice buzzed. Turtle Boy got onto the transport ship with Space Kid. Ninja Penguin was off to the right. Soon the assault began. Missiles flew everywhere, knocking Federation ships out of the sky.

"Fall back, fall back," Space Kid screamed, "and get me my armor." He jumped from the transport as he radioed Ninja Penguin that the mission was off.

BAM!

Space Kid hit the ground hard. Bullets whizzed from every direction.

"**Заморозьте** Space Kid, **вы окружены! Не двигайтесь, иначе мы будем вынуждены стрелять** (move, otherwise we will be forced to shoot)!" General Alamgir screamed.

"No!" Space Kid yelled back. Space Kid moved at the speed of light and grabbed the nukes. He stood where he once was. He screamed to the Russians, "So, does anyone want to have an old-fashioned gun duel. I'll let you shoot first."

Lieutenant Ivan Divisio stepped forward. He drew his pistol.

"Shoot!" ordered Space Kid.

Bang!

Bang!

The Lieutenant Ivan Divisio fell to the ground with a thud.

"Does anyone want to box, or are you guys still pissed about 1985," Space Kid taunted.

Sergeant Jason Ditkovitch stepped forward.

"Wow, only one person wants to beat the living daylights out of a fourteen-year-old American," Space Kid sarcastically remarked.

The sergeant punched Space Kid against a wall. For the first time, Space Kid was losing in a fight. Except, he wasn't.

"You're good," Space Kid stated, "but I'm better."

Space Kid healed his wounds. In a few punches, Space Kid was backing the Russian into a wall. He defeated the sergeant and surrendered to the Russian troops.

CHAPTER 10

SPACE KID SAT IN HIS CELL IN HIS NEW BLACK JUMPSUIT AND SAID, "Hey, you know I speak Russian, right? No? You guys are the worst."

Space Kid sat in his cell and wondered if the Russians wanted him dead. Why did he still have his phone and his gun. He checked his gun. It still had bullets in it. Should he do it?

"Give me the keys to this cell, or I'll blow both your brains out!" Space Kid threatened the guards by his cell. They fearfully handed over the keys to him.

BANG!

BANG!

Space Kid shot the guards. He took their guns and walkie-talkies. A blur whizzed past him.

"Space Pig, what do you want?" Space Kid asked.

"I'm here to get you out. We're heading back to the South Pole," Space Pig replied.

"Great," Space Kid said to Space Pig.

Space Kid took out his notepad and wrote, "IF YOU DON'T STOP MESSING WITH ME, THIS WILL BE YOU!" He stuck it onto the corpses and took them onto the *Bullet*.

"Take me to the UN. I got some packages to deliver," Space Kid re-marked.

General O'Leary walked into the UN. People looked at him with faces of disgust. He was dragging two dead bodies along behind him.

"Look at what the so-called hero did to these poor, poor Russian sol-diers," he stated.

"And I'll do it to you all as well if you don't listen to Mindwave here," Space Kid explained.

"I AM MINDWAVE! A COSMIC BEING! IF YOU DON'T HEAR WHAT I SAY, YOU WILL ALL BE FORCED TO FACE THE CONSEQUENCES! SPACE KID AND HIS ALLIES ARE NOT EVIL AND I HAVE PROOF!" Mindwave screamed.

He took out his Globe of Time and pressed Play: *"Space Kid, I'm gonna kill you slowly. Everyone you know and love will turn against you, with just a snap of my fingers. The entire world will hate you and bow down to me. Except for Switzerland, cause they're only good for cheese and choc-olate," Satan said, starting to monologue.*

"You're never going to get away with this, you deranged lunatic!" Space Kid shouted!

"I already did!" Satan boomed. Snap! "ALL HAIL SATAN! ALL HAIL SATAN!" Deaddangle, Arctic Wolf, and Shark Boy screamed.

"Ninja Penguin, NOW!" Turtle Boy shouted.

"Well, I discovered something today. I think we all have. It's that you're a cold-blooded killer!" O'Leary screamed.

"WHAT!" Space Kid jumped.

"You murdered two young men. The proof is right here," O'Leary stated, pointing to the bodies he dragged in.

"They were Russian soldiers, stationed to invade Ukraine and Poland! Also, Russia had a large nuclear arsenal, which, by the way, you guys were oblivious to," Space Kid defended.

"Let's have a vote, all who find Space Kid guilty, go to the front of the room, and if he's innocent go to the back," O'Leary stated.

Everyone got up and started to move to the front of the room. They all turned as if not sure where to go. Then they turned and embraced their hero once more. Space Kid headed back to the *Bullet*.

"You look happy," Space Pig stated.

"Let's just say the UN gave us full permission to beat a certain devil's head in," Space Kid replied.

CHAPTER 11

Space Kid, Space Pig, and Ninja Penguin all walked off the military helicopter to the sight of the new commander. Turtle Boy paused and walked off the ramp.

"It's good to have you back," the commander said, smirking.

"It's good to be back!" Space Kid replied.

"General Space Kid, the briefing is about to begin."

"Thank you," Space Kid said, nodding.

"So. Satan's base is right here. We will land our forces here. General Space Kid, we'll cover you. You and your airmen will fly here. A few 100 miles from Satan, and then land. Take whomever you need for this attack. The Federation, our Air Force, the Forces of R Turtlelandia, we don't care. Captain Turtle Boy, you and the Black Hawks will join General Space Kid here," the commander stated.

"With all due respect, I don't think that we need any more troops. Ninja Penguin, Turtle Boy, the Adventurer, Crusher, Space Pig, and I should be enough," Space Kid confidently replied. The *Bullet* whizzed through the sky. The *Adventure I* followed behind. The *Turtle* slowly followed both. A tow cable attached to the *Turtle* from the *Bullet* to help it reach 38,363.4574 mps, Mach 50!

"Prepare for nosedive, NOW!" Space Kid yelled over the comms. All the planes splashed into the Bermuda Triangle.

"Activating Heat Shield!" Space Pig yelled. Layers of the earth zoomed past the ships.

"Everyone hit the brakes in 3, 2, 1, NOW! Ninja Penguin yelled over comms. They all hit the brakes and looked at the castle of fire that was in front of them.

"Doesn't he know water puts out a fire?" Turtle Boy asked and covered the entire palace with a giant wave from his ship. Then the heroes ran into the palace. The Adventurer pulled out his gun. Shots fired. Satan only laughed. Turtle Boy and Ninja Penguin shot their ice and water at Satan. It did nothing. Satan drew his sword.

"Oh, no!" Space Kid worried.

"What is that?" Turtle Boy asked.

"That is a Vanadium Sword. The only thing that can harm Space Kid and me," Space Pig replied.

"That's right. And now I will kill you all with this!" Satan laughed with glee. Space Kid charged at Satan. *SLASH!* Space Kid screamed in agony. He looked down at his hand. It fell to the floor with a thump. *SLASH! SLASH!* Satan moved the sword so fast, Space Kid didn't realize his face had two nasty cuts on it.

"Brother!" Turtle Boy yelled. He ran towards Space Kid, but Satan got there first. He moved the Vanadium Sword at Turtle Boy and stabbed him in the gut. Space Pig and Ninja Penguin wrestled Satan away from Turtle Boy. Ninja Penguin blasted the sword to Space Kid. He picked up the sword and decapitated Satan. Space Kid ran to Turtle Boy.

"I love you, Space Kid," Turtle Boy stated.

"Come on, Jack, you'll be okay," Space Kid stated, starting to cry. It was too late. Turtle Boy was dead. Space Kid fell to his knees weeping. The Forces of Turtlelandia gathered around Space Kid and Turtle Boy. Everyone looked at Space Kid in shock. It was the first time they ever saw Space Kid cry. Space Kid picked up Turtle Boy's body and took him onto the *Bullet*.

"Space Kid, you are needed in the Medical Bay to assess your injuries," WOBOTO said.

"What's there to assess? My hand is gone!" Space Kid yelled. WOBOTO left the room. Space Kid looked down at where his hand used to be. He got straight to work on building a new hand for himself. A little while later, Space Kid walked into the common room.

"Hey, I thought your hand couldn't grow back from Vanadium," the Adventurer acknowledged.

"It can't, but since you couldn't tell the difference, that means I must have done a good job on my hand," Space Kid stated. An idea came into his head. He left the common room to go back to his lab. He had work to do.

Chapter 12

Space Kid sat at his workstation. He got all the materials he needed to build the Turtle Boy Robot.

He booted up the system that contained some of Turtle Boy's consciousness. He couldn't believe his eyes. All of Turtle Boy's turtles entered the room. Their faces lit up. They swarmed the robot of their owner and couldn't tell the difference. *I did it,* Space Kid thought.

EPILOGUE

"**T**urtle Boy, you've made it to Turtle Heaven, and the council of Turtle Gods has decided to let you live!" a voice boomed.

"Thank you," Turtle Boy said gratefully.

Turtle Boy woke up lying on the ground near Satan's Castle. He looked at his gut and saw his puncture wound was gone. He looked around and decided to take Satan's ship to get back to land.

"Wait till Space Kid sees me."